MW01487976

GINGERBREAD GETAWAY

A CHRISTMAS COZY MYSTERY

DONNA CLANCY

SUMMER PRESCOTT BOOKS PUBLISHING

CHAPTER ONE

"I can't believe after eight years your submission was finally accepted to compete in the Beltmore Hotel gingerbread competition," Denny said. "It's about time they acknowledged your talent and it's an awesome place to visit for a weekend getaway."

"It has been a long time coming. I had to pinch myself when I received the email that I was in," Kelly admitted. "It's going to be a tough competition this year. Dolly Dunlap, last year's champion, is returning to defend her title and she is one of the leading gingerbread designers in the country."

"She is good. Her work was featured in last month's Holiday Festival Magazine."

"I read that issue. Her rendition of the London Bridge decorated for the holidays was outstanding.

She will be hard to beat but I think my Westminster Abbey at Christmas may give her a run for her money."

"Speaking of money, they raised the grand prize this year to twenty-five thousand."

"I saw that. It also brought in twice as many submissions than usual. That's why I was so shocked that I got in."

"All that matters is you ARE in this year, and I will do all I can to help you win," Denny said.

"Partners. And if we win, we split the prize money," Kelly said, smiling.

"Maybe we could use the prize money to enlarge the shop. Or at least fix up the back area that is unusable right now which would double the floor area to show off some of your new clothing designs," Denny suggested.

"And some of your artwork," Kelly added.

Kelly Green had inherited a small vintage clothing shop, *Classy*, from her mother ten years ago. Two years later, Denise Parks, Denny as she liked to be called, walked in with some gowns that she wanted to consign. They hit it off when they discovered they each had a love for creating gingerbread villages. Over time, the two had become more like sisters than just best friends.

Denny rented the apartment above the shop while Kelly lived in her mom's farmhouse just down the road from the business. The shop was closed on Monday and Tuesday when Denny worked on her free-lance writing and sculpting and Kelly dabbled with sketching and sewing her own clothing designs. Any time there was an upcoming competition, the two spent their days off together cooking and packing the gingerbread pieces needed for their project. Up to this point they had only been entered in local shows.

"I'm really glad we brought all the extra ginger-bread that we did. I would have hated to run short if something goes wrong. Completion of a finished project is worth twenty percent of the final score."

"Nothing is going to go wrong. We have planned everything out right down to the finest detail. Think positive," Denny said.

"Gingerbread can be so temperamental though."

"Yes, it can, but we have everything covered. Relax will you?"

"I will when the competition is over," Kelly said, laughing.

They drove along in silence for the next half hour. Driving through the White Mountains of New Hampshire there was plenty of beautiful scenery to look at. It had snowed the day before and the mountains and hills as well as the trees were capped in white. The roads had been plowed and the bright sun had melted any residual snow or ice left on the roadways.

"Someday we have to make a trip up here during the summer. I would really love to ride the Conway Scenic Railroad and it only operates in the good weather," Denny said. "And I hear that they have awesome zip lining places to visit."

"Zip lining is all you, my friend. I'll stay right on the ground, thank you."

"Come on, where is your spirit for adventure?"

"I'm all for adventure, just not dangling hundreds of feet up in the air," Kelly said.

"I think we need to take the next exit," Denny said, checking her phone. "And the hotel is a mile up the road after we take a right off the ramp."

"We got here quicker than I thought we would. Are you ready to enter the stressful world of ginger-bread competition?"

"I hear it can be pretty tense, but yes, I'm ready. That prize money is calling my name," Denny said.

"Don't be too disappointed if we don't win. First time competitors rarely win. I would venture to say Dolly will walk away again with the money," Kelly stated.

"You never know," Denny said, pointing to the exit they needed to take.

"This place is huge," Kelly said as they pulled up to the front of the hotel.

The older section of the hotel was built in 1898. The four-floor main building where the entrance was had two wings added on to it in the early 1930's. Many famous people had stayed at the hotel over the years to enjoy the surrounding autumnal colors. The whole complex was painted in pristine white with black shutters that had a fancy scrolled B carved into the center of each one.

"I bet if these walls could talk the stories they could tell would be amazing. So much history," Kelly said. "One of the two wings had burnt to the ground twice. It was rumored that the section of land the wing had been built on was cursed by a local woman believed to be a witch. Each time the present owners had painstakingly rebuilt the wing to match the original blueprints."

"It's gorgeous. Maybe we should have done the Beltmore in gingerbread."

"Someone already did several years ago,' Kelly said, putting the car in park and shutting off the engine. "No one has done Westminster Abbey before in this particular competition."

They entered the front doors and set their suitcases down. They were in a winter wonderland indoors. The lobby area was decorated to the hilt. Ten-foot Christmas trees decorated in silver garland and all different shades of blue ornaments were scattered around the perimeter of the space. Various sized silver snowflakes sprayed with glitter hung from the ceilings and were spinning around due to the air currents that were let in during the opening of the front doors.

The grand stairway was decorated with blue and white poinsettias staggered on every other step while large fluffy blue garland loomed above them and was intertwined along the banister that led upstairs. The whole scene was breathtaking.

"May I help you?" the man behind the registration desk asked.

"We are here for the gingerbread competition," Kelly said, turning her attention to the clerk.

"Name, please?"

"Kelly Green and Denny Parks. We have reservations for a room with two queen-sized beds."

"Yes, here you are. Room 242 in the east wing. You can check in and then visit the Starry Ballroom where the competition will be held. They will instruct you how to proceed and where to unload your supplies. Sign here, please."

Kelly signed for both of them and was given two old-fashioned keys for the room.

"We don't do digital key cards here. The Beltmore is steeped in tradition and the old keys are part of that tradition," the clerk said, noticing Denny looking at hers.

"That's cool," Denny said, pocketing her key.

The clerk rang the bell in front of him.

"Take the suitcases up to room 242," he instructed the bellboy.

He loaded the suitcases onto the gold metal baggage cart and asked the two women to follow him to the elevator. No words were spoken during the ride up and the bellhop led them right to their room and unlocked the door with a master key. He brought their luggage into the bedroom and set one at the foot of each bed.

"Will there be anything else?"

"Can you tell us how to get to the Starry Ballroom from here?" Kelly asked, fishing out a ten for a tip.

"It's easy. Take the elevator back to the lobby and turn right. The ballroom is at the end of the long hallway."

"Anything else?"

"That's all, and thank you," she said, handing him his tip.

"Good luck in the competition," he said, closing the door behind himself.

"I bet he says that to everyone who gives him a good tip," Denny said, laughing.

"Probably," Kelly said in agreement.

After hanging up their clothes so the wrinkles would fall out and putting all their personal items in the bathroom, they left their room to check in for the competition. As they approached the door to the ballroom they could hear a loud voice emanating from inside.

A small crowd had gathered around two women who were having a fierce argument.

"That's Dolly Dunlap," Denny whispered to Kelly. "I wonder what they are arguing about."

"I don't know. Let's move closer."

When they got close enough, they saw a young woman, her hair held up in a bun by a very large diamond clip, in a silk three-piece suit dripping in gold and diamond jewelry. She definitely didn't look like she was here to participate in a cooking contest.

"Showing off much?" Denny whispered.

"I was the winner last year and I think I should have my choice of what display space I want," Dolly announced loudly. "I do draw in the most advertising money for this competition and should be treated in a higher regard."

"But it is tradition that the previous year's winner always displays her work up on the stage at the front of the room," the other woman countered.

"I don't want to be all the way back there. Everyone will see all the other entries before they see mine. I insist that you give me the space to the right of the door when you first enter."

"Kind of pushy, isn't she?" Denny whispered.

"Can you say diva?" Kelly replied.

"I'll have to talk to the owners before I can approve the move," the hotel employee said. "It goes against the established tradition."

"Make it quick. I don't like to be kept waiting," Dolly snapped.

"I created a monster," the woman mumbled as she passed Kelly and Denny.

"I guess we all have to wait for our space assignment thanks to the prima donna over there," the lady said that was standing next to the friends. "Karen Spenser. Are you here for the competition?"

"We are. I'm Kelly and this is my friend Denny. Have you been waiting long?"

"About a half an hour. It's all about Dolly wherever she goes."

"Have you competed against her before?"

"Many times. But it was only since she won here last year that she became unbearable to be in the same room with. This competition carries a lot of weight in the gingerbread world and when you win your name is established as a celebrity creator. But Miss Big Britches over there has taken that to a whole new level."

"I take it she is not liked very much?" Denny asked.

"Not at all. What you just witnessed is tame compared to the way she usually acts. It's almost like she knows she's going to get her way and doesn't even have to exert herself," Karen replied. "Sybil Baker started running this competition when the previous director retired after twenty-five years. She bent over backwards for Dolly last year and will probably do the same thing again. Here she comes. I bet my entry fee she has returned to tell Dolly she will get what she wants."

"Is there anyone here who would volunteer to take the spot on the stage this year?" Sybil asked the waiting crowd.

"We will," Denny answered before Kelly could even react.

"Thank you so much. I will move you up there and put the man in the spot near the door that Dolly wants into your location. There, are you happy now, Dolly?" Sybil asked nastily.

Without uttering a response or even a thank you, Dolly strutted out of the ballroom.

"Why did you volunteer to take the stage? That's almost like jinxing us, taking the winner's spot," Kelly asked her friend.

"Think about it. Dolly did us a favor by pitching her little fit. I saw the display map and we were way back in the corner squished between two other displays. Now we can shine with no one else around us."

"Your friend is right. Each space is only thirty feet wide, and you have the whole stage to create your magic on. If I had thought a little more quickly, I would have spoken up and claimed it before Denny did. I guess now that the queen is gone, the rest of us can find out where our spots are. Good luck and we will see you around." Karen said.

"Gather around, please," Sybil requested.

"As you can see each thirty-foot section has a very sturdy six by six wooden platform the center of

11

the space for you to build your displays on. You don't have to use the whole space for the structure itself, but you must cover the wood in its entirety, and it must enhance your theme. You can't just throw buffalo snow down and think the judges will approve. This is a tough competition, and the men and women rating your work are no slouches."

"Good thing we scaled down our design a little. It wouldn't have fit on the required space," Denny whispered.

"In case of a tie, I will have the final say as to who will be the winner. At the back of the ballroom to the right of the stage is the door to the kitchen for this wing. It has been shut down for this weekend and will only be used by the competitors themselves. The kitchen has been blocked off into sections and each team has been assigned one of those sections for their supplies, mixers and whatever else they have brought with them to use. No one, and I repeat no one is allowed into another competitor's section under any circumstances."

"Unless you're Dolly Dunlap," someone said from the crowd.

Kelly watched as Sybil frowned. The director knew the statement that was uttered was the way most of the competitors felt. And unfortunately, after all the talk she had heard so far about the gingerbread diva, she knew the person was probably right. Dolly did what she wanted to with no regard for anyone but herself.

"There is a loading dock at the rear of the kitchen to unload your vehicles," Sybil said, regaining her composure. "Tonight is the welcome dinner in the gold dining room at seven o'clock. You will receive your welcome packets and the full set of rules then."

"When can we unload our stuff?" Denny asked.

"You can unload your vehicles at any time during the day today, but you cannot enter the ballroom again after you check-in until the official start of the competition which will begin on Friday morning at eight a.m., and then you will have forty-eight hours to complete your submissions. The judging will take place on Sunday at ten o'clock in the morning. You will have one hour from eight to nine to put the finishing touches on your displays before you will be asked to leave for the judging."

"We got this," Denny whispered.

"Come see me for your assigned spaces and I will see everyone tonight at the dinner," Sybil announced.

"We already know where we are so let's get ahead of the game and go empty our car now before the loading dock get too crowded," Kelly said.

They left the ballroom heading for the front lobby when they recognized a shrill voice screaming from the front desk area. Dolly Dunlap was lambasting the poor desk clerk, her arms waving wildly in the air as she screamed.

"I ordered a full suite, not some tiny room where I have to look at my bed all day. Is there anybody in this hotel that can get anything right?"

"I'm sorry, Ms. Dunlap. Your assistant did not stipulate that you needed a suite, and we are fully booked this whole weekend because of the competition. There are no other available rooms at the present time," the clerk said, scanning his computer screen.

"PATRICIA!"

Dolly's young assistant stepped forward.

"Did you or did you not reserve me a suite?" Dolly demanded.

"I'm sorry. You never specified that you wanted me to book you a suite, so I booked a regular room."

"I never stay in a regular room no matter where I go. You are fired!" Dolly screamed. "Pack your bags and leave immediately."

"But…"

"But nothing. Get out of my sight. You're finished."

The young girl burst into tears and ran from the

lobby area. People looked on in disgust at the behavior of the spoiled diva in front of them. The lobby was dead silent as people waited to see what was going to happen next.

"As far as you are concerned," Dolly said to the clerk. "I will be in the bar, and I expect to be in a suite within the hour. If not, you won't have a job either."

"But I explained to you, there are no available rooms," he insisted.

"FIND ONE!"

Kelly and Denny watched as the diva, pleased with herself, strutted off and entered the bar. The lobby area that had been reduced to silence as the scene unfolded and was now a buzz. Kelly looked around for the young assistant and saw her waiting for the elevator.

"Come on," she said, grabbing Denny's arm.

"Are you okay?" Kelly asked, walking up to the crying woman.

"Yea, it was a lousy job anyway," she said, trying to manage a smile.

"No doubt," Denny mumbled.

"I'm more upset that I rode up here in Dolly's limo and have no car to get home. There are no rooms that I can book until I can rent a car on Monday."

"If you can put up with Denny's snoring, you are

welcome to stay with us. We have two queen beds. We can share one and you can have the other one," Kelly offered.

"Hey! I don't snore," Denny said in protest. "All right, maybe a little bit."

"Seriously? You would do that for me?"

"Sure. We won't be in the room much, only to sleep, so you would pretty much have it to yourself while we are working on our entry in the ballroom."

"I can't thank you enough. I have to get my personal belongings out of Dolly's room before she gets out of the bar."

"We are in room 242. I'll get another key from the desk clerk and add your name to our registration card, and we will meet you there with your things."

"There is a way I can pay you back. I am a ginger-bread designer in my own right. If you need another assistant I would be glad to help you. You are allowed up to four people on a team and if I can help you to win, I don't need or want any of the prize money. Seeing Dolly lose would be payment enough. Truth-fully, between you and me, I can't believe she even won last year. I wasn't here to fix her lame work for her."

"Why don't you sit with us at the dinner tonight as a team member. Later when we return to the room we can show you our design and see what you think of it," Kelly said.

"The submission that Dolly is using this year is mine. She couldn't design her way out of a paper bag. I can't wait to see her try to put it together without my help," Patricia said, seeing the shock on her new friend's faces. "Oh, yea, I do all the work and she takes all the credit."

"Why did you stay working for her?" Denny asked.

"She paid me very well to keep my mouth shut. But now, I no longer work for her, so I am free to tell my side of the story. And I never signed anything to prevent me from doing so."

"She'll deny everything you say," Kelly said.

"I know she will, but the evidence will be right in front of everyone when they see her final entry," Patricia said. "I will have the last laugh."

"Okay, then, we will meet you at the room," Kelly said as the elevator doors opened.

Patricia left on the elevator and the two friends headed to the front desk. Denny kept staring at her friend but wasn't saying anything. The clerk handed Kelly an extra key after she signed the registration book.

"All right. Why did you ask a complete stranger

to share our room with us? What have you got up your sleeve?" Denny asked her friend.

"There is nothing better than befriending a person who may have the inside scoop on someone you are competing with."

"I knew it. I knew you were up to something."

"And I can't wait to see the diva's face tonight when Patricia is sitting at our table and on our team," Kelly added. "She is going to freak."

"Unless this scene was all done on purpose so Patricia could spy on us and report back to Dolly. Did you think of that?" Denny asked.

"I did, but Patricia seemed to be legitimately upset for that to be true. What I don't understand is how Dolly has maintained the appearance of a creative genius in the gingerbread world of competition when it has been Patricia doing all the work. And how did she win last year? Didn't those competing against her see Patricia doing all the work?"

"If Patricia was listed on her team it wouldn't make any difference who actually did the designing or the work," Denny said. "You heard her. She was paid really well to keep her boss's secrets. Dolly could claim all the credit with Patricia's silence."

"True, but if Patricia wasn't here for the finale, how did Dolly pull off the win?"

"I don't know. I guess we will have to keep our eyes open."

They arrived at the room the same time as their new roommate. Denny moved her things off the bed closest to the door and set everything in the chair in the corner of the room. Patricia sat on the edge of the bed in complete silence.

"Are you okay?" Denny asked.

"Oh, I'm sorry. I was just thinking about finding a new job. I'm sure that Dolly will bad mouth me to anyone who will listen to her. There's not a lot of jobs out there for personal assistants especially if rumors are that you are bad at your job. Which I'm not, but I'm sure that Dolly will probably tell everyone that I am. I wish I had never taken a job with her."

"If you didn't sign anything saying you would keep her secrets then it would be in her best interest not to aggravate you by doing something stupid like that. You could ruin her."

"Yes, I could, couldn't I? Maybe it's time I strike out on my own and make a name for myself which I should have done years ago. If only Dolly hadn't paid me so well to be her lackey."

"That is now in the past," Kelly said. "Let's see how she behaves tonight when you are sitting with us."

"She's going to be madder than a wet hornet. I so appreciate you letting me stay here for the weekend, but I think I need a drink. I'm going down to the bar to relax a little before dinner."

"Don't go to the bar off the lobby. Dolly is in there," Denny said, warning Patricia.

"We are going to unload our car into the back kitchen so we will be ready to go in the morning. We'll see you at dinner."

Denny waited while Kelly brought the car around to the back of the hotel and backed it up to the loading dock. They found their assigned section and started to unload the car being very careful not to jostle the well-packed gingerbread. They had almost finished when a familiar shrill voice sounded from the loading dock.

"Whose car is this?"

"Oh boy, that sounds like Dolly again. She sure gets around," Denny said, rolling her eyes. "I bet she's complaining about our car."

"Let's go see what her problem is this time," Kelly said, carefully setting down the box that contained the smaller gingerbread sheets that would be used for the sides of the abbey.

"This car is totally empty and needs to be moved," Dolly shrieked. "How is my car supposed to be unloaded with some inconsiderate person blocking my way?"

"We just brought the last load in. There is no need to be screaming like you are," Denny said, glaring at the diva.

"This is your car? Move it, NOW!" Dolly ordered, staring down Denny as if daring her to argue.

"We'll move it when we are good and ready to move it and not before," Denny announced very loudly.

"How dare you?" Dolly demanded.

Kelly strolled over and stood extremely close to the diva. She leaned in and whispered in Dolly's ear.

"We know your secrets. Don't give us anymore grief or everyone here will know, too. Do you understand where I am coming from?"

Dolly looked at Kelly with wide eyes.

"Just move your car if you are through," she said in a normal voice, backing down. "My crew needs to bring in my supplies."

"What is your finished project going to look like without Patricia doing all the work for you?" Denny asked.

"That little witch. She has a big mouth and more than likely is telling lies to discredit me because I fired her."

"Are you saying you do all the work you claim to do?"

"Of course I do. I am Dolly Dunlap. How dare you even question me and my abilities? Wait until I find that little troublemaker. After all I did for her."

"I'm sure you mean all she did for you?" Denny questioned.

"She'll never work again when I am done with her," Dolly said, bitterly.

"If I were you, I'd let it go. She can do a lot more damage to your career than you can to hers," Kelly warned. "Make her mad and the world will know just how untalented you really are."

Dolly stared at Kelly as if she was deciding on whether or not to reply to the last statement. Instead, she turned on one foot and stormed off out the back door taking her anger out on the people that were there to unload her car.

"What a piece of work," Denny said, sighing.

"Let's go move the car and head back to the room to get ready for the dinner," Kelly suggested.

Patricia had not returned to the room yet from the bar. The two friends showered and dressed for the event and left without her. They found their assigned table and sat down. Patricia arrived to join them just as the waitress came to take their drink orders. The trio were chatting and getting to know each other a little better when a hysterical scream emanated from outside the dining room door.

They ran for the lobby to see what the screaming was all about.

CHAPTER TWO

"She's dead! Dolly Dunlap is dead!"

Sybil ran past her heading toward the ballroom. Security descended on the hysterical woman to question her. After a brief conversation, they took off in the same direction as Sybil.

"What is happening?" Patricia asked, joining the group.

"According to the woman standing over there, Dolly Dunlap is dead."

"Really? Is she sure it was Dolly?"

Before anyone could answer, Sybil and the three security guards, along with a man and woman that Kelly had never seen before returned to the lobby to talk to the woman who had found the body. Sybil had brought her a glass of white wine to calm her nerves.

The guards waited with the witness for the sheriff to arrive. Kelly and Denny stood just inside the dining room door so they could watch what was happening. Several other competitors that had been there before told the friends that the man and woman standing at the front desk were the owners of the hotel, Mary and Brian Beltmore.

"They are so young," Denny commented.

"Brian Beltmore inherited the hotel from his dad, Brian Sr. His mom passed when he was a young boy and then he lost his dad last year in a skiing accident," Patricia said.

"I wonder how Dolly died? She is way too young for natural causes, but it could have been an accidental death. Maybe she fell and hit her head," Kelly suggested.

"Not many people liked Dolly. I would lean toward someone bumping her off. Maybe she pushed her diva status a little too much and someone fought back," Patricia suggested.

Kelly looked at Patricia knowing that her time prior to arriving at the dinner was unaccounted for and that she had plenty of reasons to want Dolly Dunlap dead. Denny was having the same thoughts as they looked at each other and then at Patricia.

"What? You think I did something to Dolly?"

Patricia asked, seeing the two friends staring at her. "I was in the bar the whole time. You can check with the bartender."

"We won't, but I'm sure the police will after they find out she publicly fired you earlier today," Denny replied.

"I don't believe this. That diva is going to continue to cause problems for me even after she's dead. I'm done with this competition," Patricia said, storming off in a huff.

The sheriff arrived, his beer belly coming through the door before the rest of him did. Denny stifled a giggle as he waddled over to talk to the Beltmore's owners first before he moved on to question the woman who found the body.

"Let's move closer so we can hear what is being said," Denny said.

"You found the body?" the sheriff asked the woman who was visibly shaking and now sitting down.

"Yes, I did."

"What is your name and why are you here at the Beltmore?"

"My sister works here, and I visit every year for the gingerbread competition. My name is Shirley Baker."

"And your sister is?" the sheriff inquired.

"Sybil Baker. She is in charge of the competition."

"How did you happen to be in the ballroom? From what I was told by the owners, that area was off limits until the competition began."

"It was, I mean it is. I forgot my notes in the ballroom and went in to retrieve them. I work for the International Cuisine Magazine and cover the competition every year. I am not one of the competitors."

"Did you see anyone in the ballroom besides yourself?"

"I did not."

"Why was it so important that you get your notes at this time?"

"My editor got an anonymous tip that Dolly Dunlap was a fake. I was interviewing people during the session when they were assigned their spaces to see if I could verify the information we received. I needed my notes for the dinner tonight so I could follow up on some of the information I had already gathered."

"I bet I know who made that phone call," Kelly whispered to Denny.

The room became abuzz with the latest statement just made by the witness. Questions started to resurface as to how Dolly could have won last year's competition when she did very little work on her own submission and her team had done most of the work.

"I think people forget that anyone on the team can do the work. The person's name that appears on the submission is claiming the design is theirs," Denny whispered.

"I wonder if it was Patricia who called and tipped them off," Kelly replied. "But why would she need to kill her if she was going to ruin her career. It doesn't make sense."

Do you know how the victim was killed?" the sheriff continued.

"I'm not sure. Dolly was lying face down but there was a wooden rolling pin near her on the floor."

"Did you see anything else?"

"No, sir. I saw the blood on the floor around Dolly's head and ran from the room. I came straight out here to the lobby."

Sybil walked over and stood behind her sister, placing her hand on Shirley's shoulder.

"Sybil, can you think of anyone who would want to harm Miss Dunlap?"

"Let's put it this way. If you have all day, I can give you a list of those who despised her. She was pushy, arrogant and a total diva who had no regard for anyone but herself."

"Sounds like you didn't like her yourself," the sheriff stated.

"Not really. Dolly Dunlap was a very difficult person to work with and made life miserable for myself and all the other people she competed against."

"Deputy, put the word out no one leaves the hotel until we talk to each person. It sounds like we have a lot of people to interview," the sheriff ordered.

"Ms. Baker, do not leave the hotel, and if you think of anything else you saw, please call me," the sheriff requested, handing her his business card.

"I will."

"Please show me where the body is. Tape off the area and don't let anyone enter the crime scene," the sheriff ordered.

"The M.E. is in there taking pictures," another deputy said. "Follow me."

Kelly watched as the sheriff strolled down the hallway toward the ballroom. He didn't seem to be in any hurry to get to where he needed to be. She turned her attention to the sisters who were having a terse discussion between themselves. Sybil seemed to be lecturing or even threatening her sister. The fear on Shirley's face was evident.

"Good riddance, I say. It couldn't have happened to a nicer person," a tall, heavy-set man said, exiting the dining room.

"Ralph! That's not a very nice thing to say. A woman just died," his companion said.

"Let me tell you something. The world is not going to miss Dolly Dunlap in the least and I would like to personally shake the hand of the person who put us out of our misery."

"How do we know it wasn't you that picked off the diva, Ralph?" asked a lady following behind him. "There was no love lost between the two of you after she beat you last year in the tie breaker round."

"There never should have been a tie in the first place. I should have won outright but that doesn't mean I was mad enough to pick her off. What about you? She beat you out for the lead in that fancy holiday magazine because she caused such a stink they gave it to her instead of you."

"I guess all of us have one reason or another to despise the woman."

"All you have to do is meet her once and that's enough reason to dislike her," Denny said, voicing her opinion.

"So, the question is, who, more than anyone else, despised Dolly Dunlap enough to murder her?" Kelly pondered.

"That would be the million-dollar question," the sheriff said, coming up behind the group. "I need you people to return to the dining room as we will be calling you out one at a time to interview you."

"You heard the sheriff. We will serve you supper as planned while you wait for your turn to be interviewed," Sybil said, ushering everyone back into the dining room.

"We'll start with you, Sybil," the sheriff stated.

"Seriously? I was here in the dining room all afternoon setting up for the dinner tonight," she protested. "Many people saw me."

"You were here every minute and never left?"

"No, not every minute. I had to get supplies and check in with the kitchen staff periodically."

"Like I said. Let's go, you first," the sheriff said, walking away.

The rest of the group returned to the dining room, many grumbling along the way. People became less irritated as supper was served. Kelly looked around and it was almost as though the murder of Dolly Dunlap had never even taken place. People were laughing, drinking, and enjoying themselves. It made her sad that a person's death could be brushed off so easily.

One at a time people disappeared as a deputy would come in and get them for their interview with the sheriff. If they stayed going in the same order, Denny would be the next to leave.

"Denny, do you notice anyone missing?" Kelly asked her friend.

"No," she answered, looking around the room.

"Where is Shirley? And Sybil never returned after her interview," Kelly whispered.

"You're right. Neither of them is here. Maybe Shirley returned to her room. She did look pretty upset after she found the body."

"True. But where is Sybil? She should be here running the dinner festivities."

"Festivities. What a strange word to use after someone's death," Denny said.

"I know. It looks like it is your turn. The deputy is heading our way," Kelly said.

"They have nothing on me. I just met the woman a few hours ago," Denny said.

"You did have words with her in front of others and I'm sure that will come out. We both did," Kelly admitted.

"Miss Parks, please come with me," the deputy said, walking up behind her.

"Here goes nothing," Denny said, standing up.

Five minutes later, Denny returned to the table.

"That was fast," Kelly commented as her friend sat down.

"The sheriff wasn't too interested in what I had to say once I told him you and I had only met Dolly for the first time today. He did ask me about what happened in the kitchen but dismissed it as a simple misunderstanding."

"I guess it's my turn," Kelly said, following the deputy.

"Miss Green?" the sheriff asked.

"Yes, sir."

"Is it true you only met Miss Dunlap for the first time today?"

"Yes."

"Is it true you also had words with the victim earlier?"

"I did, but in my defense, she started it trying to push her weight around as a diva."

"I take it you didn't like her very much?"

"I don't know her enough to make a personal judgement but with everything I witnessed today I have to assume she was not liked by many people at all."

"And what did you witness?"

"She demanded to get her way in the competition assigned spaces, she fired her assistant in the middle of the lobby because she didn't like her room and she got in our faces because our car was in her way at the loading dock."

"And I was told by other witnesses that was when you whispered something to Miss Dunlap and her face showed real fear. Did you threaten to hurt her in any way?"

"I did not."

"What exactly did you say to her?"

"I told her I knew she was a fake and that her assistant did all her designing and completing of the work that she claimed as her own. I told her if she didn't back off and stop yelling, I would spill her secret to everyone in the area."

"Did she back off?"

"She did and then she took out her anger on the hotel people that had been assigned to unload her car. Denny and I left for our room to get ready for the dinner tonight."

"You did not threaten her physically in any way?"

"No, sir, I did not."

"Who is this assistant?"

"Her name is Patricia Mayes. Dolly threw her out of her room after she fired her, so she is staying in our room for the weekend as there were no other rooms available and no cars for her to rent until Monday."

"This assistant sounds like she is a viable suspect. Was she with you the whole time prior to the dinner?"

"No, sir. She said she was going to the bar for a cocktail, and I don't know where she was until she showed up at the table for dinner. And then we got in an argument, and she left."

"An argument?"

"We, Denny and I, kind of insinuated that maybe she bumped off Dolly. She vehemently denied it and stormed off."

"Thank you. Don't leave the hotel for any reason even if they cancel the competition."

"Is there talk of it being cancelled?" Kelly asked.

"The Beltmores are considering it out of respect for Miss Dunlap's death."

"That's depressing considering the truth was about to come out about Dolly being a fake and she would have had to leave the competition anyway. Maybe that's what the killer wants. If the competition is cancelled then they can slip away and never be held accountable."

"Good point. I'll talk to the owners and make sure they go on with the plans to run the event."

"If you don't mind me asking, how was Dolly killed?" Kelly asked.

"Someone whacked her with a wooden rolling pin. Not just once, but many times."

"So, someone with a lot of anger or hatred bumped her off."

"Looks like it. You are in the clear but please be careful with the assistant staying in your room. For the life of me, I don't understand why you would invite a complete stranger to stay with you," the sheriff said, shaking his head.

"At the time it seemed like a great way to spy on our biggest competitor, but that was before all the news broke about Dolly being a fake. And if what Patricia said was true about her doing all the designing and work on her boss' projects, I figured she would be a great addition to my team."

"Just be careful. Thank you for your honesty. Deputy, get the next person, please."

Kelly returned to the table just as dessert was being served. She surveyed the room and there was still no sign of Sybil, Shirley, or Patricia. The waitress came to the table asking if anyone wanted hot coffee.

"Excuse me, do you happen to know where Sybil

is?" Kelly asked the waitress as she filled her coffee cup.

"I believe she is in a meeting with the Beltmores to discuss cancelling the event."

"Thank you," Kelly said, adding sugar to her coffee.

"They are going to cancel the competition?" Denny asked.

"Not according to what the sheriff told me. He wants the event to go on to give him more time to find the killer," Kelly assured her friend.

"Sybil has made it quite clear that she doesn't want to work with a possible killer. She's afraid she might be next where she gave the win to Dolly last year," the waitress said.

"You heard her say that?" Denny asked.

"I did. I overheard her talking to her sister in the lobby right before she went in to have the meeting with the owners. But you didn't hear that from me."

"She should be next after not being able to see through the game that Dolly was playing," Ralph said from the other side of the table. "How dumb can a person be?"

"Did you see it, Ellen? I didn't," Karen Spenser asked. "I'm sorry to be so rude. This is Ellen Simms, my long-time friend and gingerbread teammate for the last twelve years."

"No, I had no idea she was a complete fake. She covered it well."

"You really are a bitter person because of losing last year, aren't you?" Denny asked Ralph. "Wishing someone harm because they were fooled by someone? That's low."

"If Dolly had to finish her own project and it was as shoddy as Patricia said it should have been, how did you end up in a tie?" Kelly asked.

"Don't ask me. Ask Sybil. She was in charge of the vote tallies and had final say as to who the winner was. I never trusted Sybil right from the beginning," Ralph complained.

"You don't trust anyone, Ralph," Karen said. "Unless you're the winner, of course. Then everything is on the up and up."

"Not true. I have lost many times and know that I deserved to lose. Every little detail counts and sometimes I miss simple little things that I shouldn't. Amateur mistakes that a seasoned professional like myself should not be making, but it happens."

"Sir, the sheriff would like to speak with you," the deputy said, tapping Ralph on the shoulder.

"He'll go right to the top of the suspect list if he

talks to the sheriff the way he talks to us," Denny said as Ralph walked away.

"The sad part is many people here feel the same way as Ralph," Karen said. "You only got a small taste of Dolly Dunlap's ego. The rest of us have been dealing with it for years especially since she won here last year."

"I know this is a prestigious competition to win, but why?" Denny asked.

"This competition features the cream of the crop in the gingerbread world, although after word gets out about Dolly being able pull off her fake win, I don't think this competition will be taken so seriously in the future," Karen replied. "The prize money is also one of the largest offered for amateur status competition."

A loud voice, declaring her innocence, came from the lobby. Kelly ran to the door just in time to see Patricia being taken away in handcuffs. The young girl was crying in between protesting her arrest.

"Okay, boys. Everyone back to the station, We have our killer," the sheriff announced.

"Why do you think Patricia killed Dolly?" Kelly asked, running up to the sheriff who had stopped at the door.

"She can't account for her whereabouts up to the

time of the murder and we caught her trying to sneak out the back door of the hotel to leave," he answered.

"She said she was in the bar. Did you check with the bartender?"

"I know how to do my job. Yes, we checked with him. He remembers giving Miss Mayes one glass of wine and then she left. I'm not going to discuss this matter any further with you," he said, opening the door and leaving without another word.

"What happened?" Denny asked when Kelly returned.

"They arrested Patricia for Dolly's murder."

"Like you said before, why would she have a reason to kill her if she could just ruin the diva's career instead. Dolly would have lost everything. Her status, the money that went with it and her life as she knew it, would have been gone. She would have been a laughingstock in her social circles. If anything, Dolly would have had more reason to kill Patricia to keep her quiet," Denny said.

"I know. It doesn't make any sense," Kelly agreed. "The truth had already been circulated, so why would Patricia kill her? There has to be another reason."

"Are you done with your dessert?" Denny asked.

"I would love to go back to the room, shower and get some shut eye."

"Sure. I need to do some research on Dolly Dunlap. I'm glad I brought my laptop with me."

"I guess I'll retire, too," Karen stated. "Good luck tomorrow. See you in the ballroom."

Denny went straight to the shower while Kelly changed into her sweats and curled up on her bed with her computer. She searched for Dolly Dunlap and many sites popped up with hits on the diva's name.

Some of the larger sites had already received the news about Dolly being a fake. Their top stories were all about the celebrity poser. Not one of the sites had picked up the story regarding the diva's death.

Kelly moved on from the gossip sites to the places where she could get the history of Dolly's life instead. Reading from several different sites, she learned that Dolly was only a year older than herself, was born in a small town in Tennessee, and had one older sister.

Hmm, I wonder why they don't list the sister's name?

Moving on, she found out that Dolly Dunlap was not the diva's real name. Her real name was Maureen Sullivan. She had taken her new name six years ago when she entered her first competition. In an interview she gave a few weeks later she explained that Dolly Dunlap had a ring to it whereas her real name was so boring.

"Did you find out any dirt on the diva?" Denny asked, coming out of the bathroom.

"Her real name is Maureen Sullivan, and she was our age. Her parents were killed in a boating accident this past summer."

"Figures. A fake name for a fake diva," Denny said, plopping down on her bed. "Is there anything real about her?"

"She has a sister, but her name isn't listed anywhere. Dolly must have distanced herself from her family when she made it big."

"Dolly was probably afraid they would ask for some of her money," Denny commented. "I wonder if her sister will inherit everything now, if they can find her, that is?"

"I don't know. Well, enough detecting for now. We need to get some sleep so we can be in the ballroom bright and early."

"I'm going to put the things Patricia left behind in the closet so I can use the bed," Denny said, grabbing the two small suitcases.

"I'm sure the sheriff will send someone by in the

morning to collect her things," Kelly said, climbing in bed.

"Let's hope we don't wake up to a notification that the competition has been cancelled," Denny said, shutting off the light.

"I think they would have let us know before now. Night."

At seven the next morning the two friends were in the dining room eating a good-sized breakfast. Having only forty-eight hours to complete their project, they didn't want to be taking time to eat various meals throughout the day. They had packed a container of snacks that they could munch on to keep themselves going while working. Competing in past competitions they knew that the time would fly by and that every second was precious.

The doors to the ballroom were opened at eight o'clock. The teams were asked to take their places in their assigned spaces while Sybil went over the last section of the rules. She seemed extremely nervous. Never looking at anyone in particular, she stared at the ceiling while she spoke and continually flipped the folder she was holding over and over in her hands.

"Looking at Sybil, you would think she was the killer. She's a wreck," Denny whispered to Kelly.

"I wonder if she's hiding something or if she

really believes she might be next," Kelly replied. "She did want the event cancelled."

"You may begin," Sybil announced.

The teams ran toward the kitchen door at the rear of the room while Sybil went in the opposite direction out the front door of the ballroom. The kitchen was abuzz with excitement. Instructions were being yelled out to team members and the empty stainless-steel tables were quickly filling up with slabs of ginger-bread and frosting supplies. Most teams had four members, but there were a few that had only two workers like Kelly and Denny's team.

"Keep your eyes and ears open as the day progresses," Kelly said as they carried containers of gingerbread that would be the foundation of their abbey.

"Can't we let the sheriff take care of that? We really need to concentrate on what we are doing because I believe we stand a real chance of winning this thing now that Dolly has been eliminated. And I do mean taken out of the competition not taken out permanently."

"Unfortunately, I think many of the people here are thinking the same thing. That's what makes this so scary. The killer could still be in this room with us," Kelly said, mixing a batch of stiff consistency royal icing to start putting the base of the abbey together. "Would you please go get the smaller side walls and we can start putting this thing together?"

"If we spend today putting together the structure, we can let it dry overnight and then do the piping and decorating tomorrow when we know the abbey is solid. I think twelve hours for each phase is ample time, don't you?"

"It's perfect and anything we forget we can complete in the last hour on Sunday before the judging."

"I wonder who the judges are this year. I really hope that none of them are returning from last year."

"Ralph was saying that they are all new this year. They brought them in from New York City where they just finished judging the Times Square competition. He said he knew five of the six and they were fair and very competent in their judging standards."

"Well, if they got Ralph's stamp of approval, they must be on the up and up," Denny said, chuckling. "And he won't be able to cry foul when we beat him."

"You're awfully confident. Have you looked around at some of the displays that people have started? They're pretty big."

"Size doesn't matter. It's the finished project and its fine details that will win this competition. We have gone over our blueprints so many times I can't help but feel confident that we will win."

"The base is in place. Shall we raise the walls?" Kelly asked. "If we do the larger ones first we can go make the wreaths and candles for the windows while they set. Then we can move on to the roof and the twin steeples on the front of the church.."

"You can work on the little stuff. I'll temper some dark chocolate and start piping the fence that will surround the abbey. I made a template to follow so all the fence sections will be identical."

"I saw your templates for the stained-glass windows and the clocks on the front of the abbey. They will be stunning when we brush them in gold dust and add the colors that are needed."

An hour later the friends had completed the main building of the abbey, minus the top sections of the two towers on the front of the church and laid the side foundation for the smaller sanctuary. As they returned to the kitchen area, they walked slowly checking what the other teams were working on for their projects.

Some structures they recognized immediately like Buckingham Palace and The White House. But there were some projects that even though the buildings had basically been assembled, they were still unrecognizable. Most of the teams were following the same routine as Kelly and Denny. They had done their basic assembling and now had returned to the kitchen to work on the smaller detail work.

There were sixteen competing teams. Kelly watched Karen and Ellen work and how they knew exactly what the other one needed when they needed it. They were a well-oiled machine, and it was obvious they had worked together over a long period of time. They had submitted the Queen Mary decked out for Christmas with a lit gang plank attaching the ship to the dock. Kelly knew that bending the ginger-bread to form the ship was a lot harder than creating a building with straight walls and she admired Karen for her bravery in attempting this design.

Hours were spent with their heads down creating the smaller details needed for their piece. At the end of the first day Kelly and Denny felt confident they had put in a good days work and were where they needed to be in their schedule. As they were covering up the trays with the chocolate fences on them, Sybil entered the room and was walking around checking out the progress of the teams competing.

Just before she reached the friend's area, the sheriff and two of his deputies entered the kitchen searching for someone. They spotted Sybil and headed right for her. After a few short words, they handcuffed her and led her out of the kitchen. She didn't react in any way but allowed herself to be led away quietly and quickly.

"Maybe I was right. Sybil might have been the killer," Denny said.

Moments later, the hotel owners, Mary and Brian, entered the kitchen and asked for everyone's attention. The room became silent as everyone was waiting for them to say the event had been cancelled.

"It has been brought to our attention that last year's competition had been rigged and the final results had been manipulated by our own employee, Sybil Baker. I will not go into the details as it is still under investigation by the sheriff. I am here to tell you that this year's competition will continue but under new leadership. One of our New York judges has kindly stepped forward to take Sybil's place."

"I knew it! I knew something was fishy last year," Ralph bellowed.

"Ralph, calm down and be quiet," his wife said.

"But I should have won last year. I should have asked to see the judge's tally cards but I didn't. That prize money should have been mine."

"Anyone in last year's competition can make the same claim as you, Ralph," Karen stated. "How do we know that you were even at the top spot in the tie?

Sybil could have picked someone's name out of a hat, you don't know."

"We are looking into all the allegations, but as we do, please continue to complete your projects with the full knowledge that the judging will be on the up and up this year as I myself will be overseeing the tally sheets."

The Beltmores left the kitchen area. People were not moving, still taking in the news that they had just received.

"Well, this just gets more and more interesting as each hour passes, doesn't it?" Denny asked. "I wonder why Sybil rigged the contest for Dolly to win?"

"From what I heard, Sybil and Dolly split the prize money," Karen said.

"And where did you hear that?" Kelly asked. "And if you heard that, why didn't you step forward and say anything?"

"I think it was you that told me, wasn't it, Ellen? Besides, nothing could be proven as all the ballots were destroyed after the competition."

"And where did you hear it from, Ellen?" Kelly asked.

"I heard mention of it at another competition months later. You know how rumor mills work.

People will say anything when they don't win and want to make the person who did win look bad. And any chance to make Dolly the diva look bad was jumped on."

"Why did you come back if you knew Sybil was still in charge and Dolly would be competing again?" Kelly asked.

"I figured they wouldn't be brazen enough to try to pull off the same thing this year, so I came back. I assumed other people heard the rumors and would be watching the two as carefully as I would be."

"Looking around the room, I don't think many people knew what happened here last year. They seem to be in shock over the news," Kelly said. "I'm sure if Ralph even had an inkling of what took place he would have filed a grievance with the hotel."

"So, did Sybil kill Dolly so she couldn't testify against her for embezzlement?" Kelly asked. "Or maybe, Dolly was trying to force Sybil into letting her win again this year and Sybil didn't want anything to do with it."

"Could be," Karen replied, walking back to her own section in the kitchen. "Everything the diva got, she deserved."

"I need to do more research on our murder victim.

Let's grab some supper and bring it back to the room," Kelly suggested.

"I have a better idea. Let's use room service. I have always wanted to stay at a hotel that had room service and be able to use it," Denny said.

They finished covering up their trays and were leaving the kitchen when Karen asked them if they wanted to join her and Ellen for supper. Kelly declined and said they would be eating in their room.

"Let's go, Sully. I'm famished. We haven't eaten all day," Ellen said, linking her arm in Karen's as they walked away.

Kelly left the ordering of room service up to Denny as she opened her computer to do more research on Dolly Dunlap and her family. A quiet knock on the door a half an hour later was answered by Denny and a white curtained cart was wheeled into the room. Denny tipped the man and closed the door.

"Did you order everything off the menu?" Kelly asked, looking at the number of cloches on the cart.

"No, but I could have because everything sounded so good. I ordered shrimp cocktails for both of us, steak for you and broiled scallops for me. I figured we could share and have a surf and turf supper. And I ordered caramel and blueberry cheesecake for dessert.

You can pick which one you want as I will gladly eat either one."

"Did you hit the lottery and not tell me?"

"I saved up for this weekend for a long time and I am going to treat myself and you. It's not often we get to eat like this."

"Let's dig in," Kelly said, lifting several of the larger cloches.

They used the cart as a buffet area and ate at the small round table in the corner of the room. Denny had also remembered to order a bottle of Zin. They toasted to a good day of work and enjoyed their meal.

"I think I have been going at this all wrong," Kelly said, plopping a scallop into her mouth.

"What are you talking about?"

"I think instead of researching Dolly's sites, I need to be looking into her parents and their business."

"They had a business?"

"Remember I told you they died in a boating accident? Well, apparently they owned a charter business, and they were out on their own boat when it went down in a freak storm."

"That's terrible."

"Yes, it is. Maybe there is a mention in one of the

obituaries or news articles of who the sister is and if Dolly attended the services for her parents."

"Why are you so interested in the sister? The killer has to be either Patricia or Sybil."

"I don't know. Something is gnawing at me. I don't think it was Patricia as she had other avenues to destroy Dolly's career and had already started to do so. Now Sybil on the other hand had lots of reasons to bump off Dolly."

There was another knock at the door. Denny answered it to see Patricia standing in the hallway. She looked terrible. Her eyes were swollen, her face was blotchy, and her hands were shaking.

"Patricia, what are you doing here?" Denny asked, not letting her in.

"The sheriff said I was free to go. They dropped the charges against me when I explained that I panicked and tried to leave the hotel because I knew I would be looked at because of Dolly firing me. I was truthful and told them everything."

"Everything?" Kelly asked, walking up to the door.

"I guess I'm the reason they went after Sybil. I told them about the fixed winner last year and that Dolly was insisting it happen again this year."

"You knew about all that?"

"I did."

"Why didn't you say anything to us about it?" Kelly asked.

"I was going to use it as leverage against Dolly. I knew she was going to badmouth my work ethics and I figured I could hold that against her if she did."

"Did you ever tell anyone you knew the fix had happened?"

"No, nobody, but I do believe her sister knew. I think Dolly had bragged about her ability to make people do what she wanted them to do when she went home to attend her parents' services. Dolly and her sister never got along and hadn't spoken to each other for years before the death of their parents. I guess you could call it a sort of a forced reunion."

"Do you know her sister's name?" Kelly asked.

"No. Dolly's sister was a subject that was off limits to discussion. As a matter of fact, her whole family was. She never acknowledged any of them. I wasn't even allowed to go to Tennessee when Dolly traveled home."

Denny stared at Patricia suspiciously.

"I didn't kill her, I swear," Patricia said, sobbing.

"Have you had anything to eat today?" Kelly asked.

"No."

"Come on, we'll share our dinner with you. Your suitcases are in the closet if you want to shower before you eat."

Denny looked at her friend with wide eyes. She didn't understand how her friend could just open the door and let a possible killer in their room. Kelly made the 'I'll tell you later face' that she had made so many other times in their friendship. She trusted her friend, so she stepped aside and let Patricia in.

Patricia grabbed the smaller of the two cases and locked herself in the bathroom. The friends could hear her crying through the locked door.

"I'd be crying too if I had the kind of day she probably did," Kelly said, sitting back down at the table.

"Maybe you trust her and don't think she did it, but I am still unsure. Why would you invite her back into our room?"

"What better way to keep track of her than to have her right here with us?"

"Did you stop to think she could pick us off in our sleep?" Denny insisted.

"You've watched too many forensic shows. What possible reason would she have to kill us? We only met her yesterday and we are the only ones who have befriended her."

"I'm taking the window side. You can sleep closest to her tonight. And don't think I will get much sleep, so I'll probably be cranky all day tomorrow," Denny said.

"You'll get plenty of sleep. Patricia didn't do it. I have a gut feeling and usually my feelings are spot on," Kelly insisted.

"Now who has watched too many detective shows? Feelings, really?" Denny asked.

"I'm done eating and am going to hop on my computer. You can pick which cheesecake you want before Patricia comes out."

"Just because you're letting me have my choice of dessert doesn't mean I forgive you for letting her stay here tonight," Denny said, grabbing the caramel cheesecake.

"You'll be fine."

The only sound in the room was the sound of running water coming from the bathroom. Denny couldn't take the quiet, so she turned on the television and started to surf the channels for something she was interested in watching.

Kelly pounded away on the keyboard. Every once in a while she would stop to read what was on the screen. At one point she let out a gasp.

"What's up?"

"There is a story in The Tennessee Tribune on the boat accident. The reporter writes that the parents' deaths should never have happened. They were within days of losing their boat and their business, so they took on the extra charter because they needed the cash for their bank payment to hold off the foreclosure. The weather was iffy, and they shouldn't have ventured out. They got caught in a fierce thunderstorm while out on Norris Lake and didn't return to the dock later that evening. The boat was found three days later in seventy feet of water with the bodies inside the cabin. The report says it looked like the boat had been hit by lightning."

"Dolly had money, why didn't she help her parents?" Denny replied.

"Because Dolly didn't help anyone but Dolly," Patricia said, coming out of the bathroom.

"Did you know about the situation her parents were in?"

"No, I didn't. Dolly distanced herself from her southern roots. It's almost like she was embarrassed about where she hailed from."

"Help yourself to the food."

"I'm just going to have a little of the cheesecake and then go to bed. It's been a long day and my nerves are shot. If that's okay, I mean."

"I'm going to sleep, too," Denny said, pulling back the bedspread.

"I have a few more things to check out but I'll stay at the table, so the light of the screen won't bother you," Kelly said.

For the next two hours, Kelly continued to search the computer for any local articles pertaining to Dolly or her family. She wasn't sure what she was looking for, but she would know it when she saw it. After sifting through many articles and interviews given by the family members and friends, Kelly finally found what she was looking for. Two pictures told the whole story.

"I think I know who killed Dolly," she whispered.

CHAPTER THREE

Kelly was anxious to get to the ballroom the next morning. She had called the sheriff and requested that he be there at nine o'clock. Denny had been right. She got no sleep and was moving at the pace of a slug. When the friends finally left the room, Patricia was still sleeping.

The ballroom was buzzing with speculation as to why the sheriff was there. Kelly walked in and went directly to the sheriff and had a long conversation with him. The competitors were all standing in their assigned spots waiting for the morning instructions before they started to work. The sheriff walked around the room and stopped in front of Karen and Ellen's space.

"And what can we do for you today, sheriff?" Karen asked.

"You can come with me to the station and answer some questions," he replied.

"I'm afraid that is quite impossible. Today is the last day we have to complete our projects for the final judging tomorrow morning. I will gladly come to the station and answer any questions you have at the conclusion of the competition," Karen said.

"I think you need to answer the sheriff's questions now, Sully," Kelly said.

Karen Spenser froze. Her eyes grew wide with the knowledge that they knew who she really was.

"Karen Sullivan. I assume Spenser is your married name? You are Dolly's sister, are you not?" the sheriff asked.

"I am," she stuttered.

"You knew that Dolly and Sybil had fixed the contest last year. She bragged about it when she returned to Tennessee and you weren't going to let her win again, were you? So, you killed her," the sheriff said.

"I may have hated my sister, even despised her, but I didn't kill her," Karen said, defiantly.

"But you knew your parents asked for Dolly's help.

They asked her to loan them the money to help save their business and she laughed at them. The local newspapers blamed Dolly for your parent's deaths because if their famous daughter had helped them they wouldn't have been out on the lake that day," Kelly said.

"That is true. I blamed Dolly, too. If the contest hadn't been rigged I might have stood a chance of winning and I could have helped my parents with the prize money. It was Dolly's ego and lust for money that killed my parents. But I will say it again. I did not kill my sister."

"No, I don't think you did," Kelly announced. "But someone else was killed in the accident, weren't they, Ellen?"

Ellen glared at Kelly.

"Go on," the sheriff requested.

"Ellen's brother was the first mate on the boat. He had been working for Dolly's parents for almost two years and he went down with the boat also."

Ellen continued to glare at Kelly not saying a word.

"You killed Dolly, didn't you, Ellen?"

"I did no such thing."

"But you did, and I have the proof it was you."

"You have nothing because I didn't do it."

"Sheriff, did you bring the crime scene photos with you?"

"They are right here," he said, handing the photos to Kelly.

"Earlier in the day when Dolly was causing the scene about her assigned space, there was a discussion about how overdressed she was for being at the hotel to cook. She had on a lot of jewelry that glimmered under the lights when she waved her arms about."

Ellen pulled her sleeves down and slid her arms behind her back but no one but Kelly noticed her doing it.

"One piece caught my eye. It was a diamond bracelet with a gold gingerbread man fashioned as the clasp. I thought the piece was stunning."

She pulled a particular photo out of the evidence folder.

"These are the pictures that were taken by the M.E. right after the murder. As you can see, Dolly is in the same suit with the same jewelry on with one exception. The photo of her wrist shows the diamond bracelet is not on her arm and was found nowhere on the floor if it had fallen off in the struggle."

Ellen turned white. All the color drained from her face, but she still didn't say anything.

"Only the person who killed Dolly Dunlap could have the bracelet. Sheriff, if you care to look at Ellen's wrist, I'm sure you will find the bracelet there. I saw it yesterday as she linked arms with Karen."

"Hold out your arms, please," the sheriff instructed.

Ellen stood there, frozen.

"Why, Ellen? Why did you do it?" Karen asked. "We were making our own name in the competition world. You had enough money to be comfortable and to be able to travel anywhere we needed to go for the competitions."

"It wasn't about the money; it was about my brother. He was only twenty-one when he died. He had his whole life ahead of him until your ego driven sister couldn't find it in her heart to help her own parents. They never should have been out on the lake that day. It's all her fault that Jimmy is gone. All her fault…"

"How did you know it was me, besides the bracelet, I mean," Ellen asked as the sheriff put on the cuffs.

"I saw your picture in The Tennessee Tribune. You and Karen were standing at the entrance to the cemetery and stopped for an interview with a reporter. In the interview you stated that you would get even with the person who caused your brother's death without mentioning any specific name, Kelly replied. "Also, you called Karen, Sully. I didn't put it together at first but then I remembered that Sully is used a lot as a shorter version for Sullivan, so I did some research. And then I saw the bracelet on your wrist."

"She got what she deserved and I'm not sorry I did it," Ellen yelled as she was taken away out of the ballroom. "I did it for my brother. I'm sorry, Karen. I never meant to hurt you."

"I can't believe Ellen hid her hatred for my sister from me all this time. I thought she had moved on," Karen said, sobbing. "My whole family is gone and now my best friend. I am withdrawing from the competition. I need some time alone to deal this whole mess."

"If you need to talk, I'm in room 242," Kelly offered.

"Okay, people, I know a lot has happened over the last couple of days, but it is time to buckle down and get to work. You have all day today and one hour tomorrow morning."

The competitors scampered to the kitchen to get to work, Kelly and Denny right behind them. At eight o'clock that evening, the abbey was completed. The two towers had been added to the front of the building and stood majestically over the smaller sanctuary building. The wrought iron fence done in chocolate was added last surrounding the whole piece. Every minute detail had been addressed and they were ready for the judging.

After eating a late dinner, they went to bed. Neither of them could sleep as their nerves were working overtime while waiting for the judging. Denny dozed off sometime after midnight and Kelly sometime around three.

They returned to the ballroom the next morning for the last hour of detail work. The friends found a few small items that they addressed and then walked around looking at the other entries. Karen's space had been cleared and there was nothing but an empty table where the ship used to sit. They agreed that the competition would be stiff and pitied the judges who had to make the final decision.

The ballroom was cleared while the judges walked around and tallied their decisions. Forty-five minutes later they were called back to the ballroom for the all-important announcement.

Brian Beltmore hopped up on the stage with the judge's rating cards in his hand.

"I have overseen the whole judging process. These are the judge's tallies which will be kept in the hotel safe until next year in case there are any questions raised as to their authenticity."

"Good idea," Denny whispered.

"Here we go. In third place for her rendition of Central Park at Christmas time is Penny Silverton."

A round of applause greeted her as she went to the stage to get her yellow ribbon.

"First place and second place were separated by only one point this year. Second place for their stunning display of Westminster Abbey goes to Kelly Green and Denny Parks."

"Darn," Denny said as they walked up to the stage. "One stupid point between us and the money."

"There's always next year. At least we will be recognized in the International Cuisine Magazine so our name will get out there," Kelly replied.

"And first place honors and the check for twenty-five thousand dollars goes to…," Brian paused for a dramatic affect. "Ralph Currier for his way out and wacky rendition of Whoville. Doctor Seuss would be proud. Congratulations to all and start those designs for next year."

A small crowd gathered around Ralph congratulating him on his win. He waved Kelly and Denny over to where he was standing.

"I wanted to thank you for lifting the veil of dread

that was hanging over the competition and allowing people to be able to concentrate on what they were doing."

"You are so welcome, and your piece was outstanding," Kelly replied.

"Your abbey was too, but one point is one point. I'll take the win. I hope you will be back next year," Ralph said.

"Oh, don't you worry. We'll be back and next year we will win by one point over you," Denny said, laughing.

"The challenge is on," Ralph said, smiling.

"Yes, it is, and hopefully it will not include another murder in the ballroom," Kelly replied. "Now, let's all go have lunch together."

Made in United States
North Haven, CT
04 January 2024

47071061R00050